To all my family on this continent
and the other, and Paula and Brian.
And, Eee-Moo–you made it!

—A. D.

Everything, always
Leny & Charlie

—B. W.

A Paula Wiseman Book
Simon & Schuster Books for Young Readers
New York London Toronto Sydney New Delhi
SIMON & SCHUSTER BOOKS FOR YOUNG READERS
An imprint of Simon & Schuster Children's Publishing Division
1230 Avenue of the Americas, New York, New York 10020
Text copyright © 2019 by Annika Dunklee • Illustrations copyright © 2019 by Brian Won
All rights reserved, including the right of reproduction in whole or in part in any form.
SIMON & SCHUSTER BOOKS FOR YOUNG READERS is a trademark of Simon & Schuster, Inc.
For information about special discounts for bulk purchases, please contact
Simon & Schuster Special Sales at 1-866-506-1949 or business@simonandschuster.com.
The Simon & Schuster Speakers Bureau can bring authors to your live event. For more information or to book an event,
contact the Simon & Schuster Speakers Bureau at 1-866-248-3049 or visit our website at www.simonspeakers.com.
Book design by Chloë Foglia • The text for this book was set in Cochin.
The illustrations for this book were rendered digitally. • Manufactured in China
0719 SCP • First Edition
2 4 6 8 10 9 7 5 3 1
Library of Congress Cataloging-in-Publication Data
Names: Dunklee, Annika, 1965- author. | Won, Brian, illustrator.
Title: Eee-Moo / Annika Dunklee ; illustrated by Brian Won.
Description: First edition. | New York : Simon & Schuster Books for Young Readers, [2019] | Summary: Mistakenly
believing himself to be an emu, a newly-hatched platypus sets out on a long journey,
using various forms of transportation and aided by new friends, to reach Australia.
Identifiers: LCCN 2018039840| ISBN 9781534401747 (hardcover) | ISBN 9781534401754 (e-book)
Subjects: | CYAC: Platypus—Fiction. | Mistaken identity—Fiction. |
Voyages and travels—Fiction. | Animals—Fiction. | Friendship—Fiction.
Classification: LCC PZ7.1.D8626 Ee 2019 | DDC [E]—
dc23 LC record available at https://lccn.loc.gov/2018039840

Eee-Moo!

Words by
Annika Dunklee

Pictures by
Brian Won

One day, in a little town not so far away,
a platypus egg was found
and brought to the local zoo.

But suddenly . . .

and then . . .

the egg rolled, and rolled, and rolled

until . . .

CRAAAACK!

POP!

EEE!
squealed the pig.

MOO,
bellowed the cow.

"Eee-Moo!" announced the platypus a moment later.

"He's an emu, of course," said the horse.

"What's an emu doing here?" asked the owl. "He's very far away from home."

"He should take a bus," suggested the chicken.
"At the very least," confirmed the owl.

X

AUSTRALIA

HOME ~~OF~~ EEEMOO

So, Eee-Moo the emu, who was actually a platypus,
set off on his journey to Australia,
land of the emu—home to Eee-Moo?

Eee-Moo took a bus . . .

BUS TOUR

then a ferry . . .

followed by a train . . .

then a moped . . .

then a rickshaw . . .

and finally, an airplane.
Until at last, Eee-Moo arrived in Australia.

As Eee-Moo stood waiting for a cab, along bounced a kangaroo.

"'Ow ya goin'?" the kangaroo greeted Eee-Moo.

"Eee-Moo!" replied Eee-Moo.

"You wanna see the emus? Hop in, young fella— I'll take you there myself!"

Just then, a kookaburra flew by overhead. "Hellooo, down there!" he called. "Where are you off to?"

"Emus!" the kangaroo called back. "This little fella's looking for emus!"
"That's just where I'm headed! I'll take him the rest of the way."

up . . .

went Eee-Moo
and the kookaburra.

up . . .

Up . . .

But Eee-Moo was
way too heavy.

Down . . .

down . . .

down . . .

went Eee-Moo.

But, as luck would have
it, he was dropped *right*
into an emu farm below.

"Well, hello. Who might you be?" asked one of the emus.

"Eeeee-Moooo!" declared Eee-Moo, ready to receive all his hugs.

"Yes, *I'm* an emu, but what are you?" asked the emu.

Eee-Moo looked around and suddenly noticed he didn't look anything at all like an emu.

Eee-Moo's eyes began to well up with tears. He had taken a bus, train, ferry, moped, rickshaw, airplane, kangaroo, *and* kookaburra, only to find out he didn't belong here after all. He had traveled all this way for nothing.

"Now, just hold on a minute . . ." piped up a koala, who had been listening to everything in a nearby eucalyptus tree. "I think I have an idea. Hop on board and you'll see what I mean."

The koala, with Eee-Moo on his back, walked along a
dusty path until they reached the edge of a stream.
"We've been looking everywhere for you!" cried Eee-Moo's
mother and father, running toward him with open arms!

So, Eee-Moo the emu, who was actually a platypus, from the little town not so far away—which as it turns out was quite far away—had taken a bus, train, ferry, moped, rickshaw, airplane, kangaroo, kookaburra, *and* koala, to find home.

But, Eee-Moo realized something was missing—
all of his friends who helped him along the way.

So he invited them
for a visit.

WELCOME